EDEN *miniatures*

THE TAPE

Optimist

© 2018 by FREI

The Tape

First Edition

The Tape was first published as part of *EDEN by FREI*
– *a concept narrative in the here & now about the where,
the wherefore and forever* at *EDENbyFREI.net*

All rights reserved. No part of this publication may be reproduced,
stored in a retrieval system or transmitted in any form or by any
means, electronic, mechanical, photocopying, recording or otherwise
without the prior permission of the publisher or in accordance with
the provisions of the Copyright, Designs and Patents Act 1988.

The right by FREI to be identified as the author of this
work has been asserted by them in accordance with
the Copyright, Designs and Patents Act 1988.

ISBN: 978-1-64255-166-2

Optimist Books by Optimist Creations

optimistcreations.com

Divestment	1
Origin	7
Edinburgh	15
Paris	27
Songs & Charades	37
Towards Italy	45
Helvetia	61
{Bereavement}	73
Les Grands Amours	87
London	95

The Tape

Divestment

I find a cassette tape, unlabelled.

I'm in the process of divesting myself of accumulated clutter that has started to clog up my life, in preparation for a renovation of my flat, and most of the tapes are being at long last thrown out now. Some—those bought as albums and undamaged—go to the charity shop, practically all others, with the exception only really of some mixtapes which have memories attached to them and therefore some sentimental value, go in the bin: I hold on to less than half a dozen, which is me being ruthless. I reckon.

The unlabelled tape nearly lands in the bin liner unexamined, but it intrigues me as there are almost no tapes that don't have anything written on them at all, even if on some of them the writing has long faded and become illegible. I take it out of its case and put it in the machine I still own to play tapes, which I haven't used in more than a decade.

I hear a young voice with a not particularly strong but clearly discernible accent, a little measured, a little studied, a little over-enunciated, declare: "All right, here we go: Europe Tour 1988, The Spoken Diary." I'm listening to myself, nearly thirty years ago. And I hear myself say: "This is my first experience of this kind as well, so we just have to try it out." My language has not yet acquired any idiom, and Germanisms linger, sometimes prevail.

"Nothing of what's going to be said is going to be edited in any way, I promise myself that, so that when I'll be listening to it in two or three or five years, ten years, I'll feel genuinely embarrassed." Not embarrassed, my friend, so much as astounded. I sound to me like any young man from the past. I recognise myself, but in the way that I would recognise a friend from that time, someone I knew, a little. Not someone I knew well, let alone someone I was. I don't remember the process of recording this, but I do recall having made The Tape. The memory is curious, brittle, alien.

The 'Europe Tour', it transpires, starts in Edinburgh, with a first diary entry on Monday 14th August (which I pronounce *Oggust*, and that does embarrass me now a little, though it also endears me to me) at 2:15 in the afternoon, a time by which I announce, with a hint of pride lacing my voice, that I haven't slept in about twenty-four hours. I've had a "very pleasant conversation" with two Americans on the train, and upon arrival availed myself of the services of the Tourist Information Office, who have booked me into this "guest house." Saying "guest house," I sound bemused, almost baffled at my own predicament.

Having settled into my room, which, apparently, has high ceilings and is also "pleasant," I've headed out and bought myself tickets to three shows at the Fringe Festival, the first one starting at 4:15pm.

"I've just eaten this strange, slobbery pizza, which was incredibly cheap though," I note, and "people here have time, and they let you know they do, which can be charming as well."

I describe with awe the light of the city in London, pulling out of King's Cross Station at six thirty in the morning, and call Edinburgh "wonderful" and unlike anything I'd seen before; but I also remark that the drawback of this place is the weather: I'd already spotted someone wearing a fur coat at the height of summer, though I make no reference to 'nae nickers' – perhaps I'm not yet familiar with the expression.

"I seem to be sounding a bit *blasé*, hearing myself over the headphones, but I'll have to get used to that, I presume." And I'm not joking. Today, I sound to me like a young arrival's idea of a latter day Noël Coward, and it hits me: I still own the silver cigarette case I used to use at that time, quite without irony.

Hearing this now, I sense there's a fair chance that it might get me to know me better, and I resolve to listen to myself speak to me from the past...

Origin

I was born in Manchester in June 1964 into a Swiss family, and I have never been in any doubt that both these facts are of defining significance.

Had I been born in Manchester into an English family, I would most likely have grown up either in Manchester, or if not there then somewhere else in Britain, and if not that then at any rate in an English-speaking household. Had I been born in Switzerland or anywhere else, I might never have developed my powerful affinity to England and the English language.

As it turned out, I grew up as the 'English Boy' in a Swiss family in Switzerland, because soon after my birth—a mere six weeks—I was carried aboard a plane in a red wicker basket and flown, together with my brother and two sisters, to Basel, where my arrival was greeted with jolly brass bands and a splendid fireworks display. It would please me to think that the good people of Basel were thus celebrating my homecoming, but it just happened to be Swiss National Day, 1st August; and also it wasn't in that sense a homecoming.

Because although I was a fiercely patriotic child, my loyalties then were always almost evenly divided between Switzerland and England, with Switzerland slightly having the edge, and as I grew into my teenage years the balance began to tip in favour of England.

But more important than that—and also perhaps more curious—although I had really done all my growing up in Arlesheim, a beautiful, picturesque and particularly peaceful and well cared-for village outside Basel, and in Basel itself, where I went to school, I never actually really felt 'at home' there.

I felt at home in London the moment I set foot in it when my parents took me and the younger of my two sisters there for the first time: this, I thought, is where I want to be. I was twelve. From then on in, I returned to London every year at least once, often twice, at first staying with a friend of the family, then with friends I made there during my visits, or at a hostel or a cheap hotel, and from as early as sixteen I started talking about moving to London.

I finished school, spent a year enrolled at Basel University, and then left. I took with me two suitcases, one black, one red—neither of them had castors back then—and I'd wanted to buy a one-way ticket to

THE TAPE

London. The slightly bored—too bored, I thought: I'm moving to London! That's *exciting!*—travel agent laconically told me she could sell me a one-way ticket, but that it would be more expensive than buying a return and simply not coming back. It irked me, this, but I was twenty-one and I had to make the money I'd earned as a security guard over the previous few months last, so I opted for the more economical offer and bought a return, the outbound on the 1st August: Swiss National Day, precisely 21 years after I'd arrived in Switzerland.

Of course, I didn't use the return leg, I let it lapse: I did not go back. Not, it seems, until now, three years later, when my 'Europe Tour 1988' took me, after Edinburgh, from Grenoble to Vicenza back to Chur and then Basel, where I saw first my sister, then my parents, my brother and his two sons (the older my godson), my other sister, and many friends from the then recent past.

The way I talk about it all on The Tape does not feel 'recent' though, I talk about having lived in London now for three years as a big chunk of my life, and it is a big chunk at that time: it's all of my adult life so far.

My delivery on The Tape is measured, often very quiet (mostly out of consideration: I seem to be recording the majority of my entries very late at night; that's one thing that hasn't changed: I'm still a night owl…), and I choose my words carefully, though not always correctly. I refer, for example, to a part of the trip as being 'exhaustive' when I mean 'exhausting,' and I keep calling things 'well done' when I mean they are either well made or simply good. I forever seem a bit bemused and a bit *blasé,* absolutely, and also a little in awe; I marvel, but I don't gush; I describe things as 'fantastic,' but say the word as you would say the words 'flower bed,' and often qualify things towards moderation. I sound to me now almost like someone who's rediscovering his language, who's searching hard, and sometimes finding, sometimes just missing, the right expression, who's grappling, without really knowing it, for a lost code, but enjoying the process of slow rediscovery.

There is good evidence now that you pick up a great deal as an unborn child in your mother's womb; you make out sounds and noises, and you start recognising them and responding to them long before you are able to make any sense of them. I always loved English as a child, and as a young teenager I became very 'good' at it (though I also wildly overestimated my abilities).

Perhaps—and I do mean this 'perhaps' as a distinct possibility, it's not here merely for a rhetorical purpose—the familiarity that nine months as a growing foetus and then six weeks as a newborn baby in an English-speaking environment engendered in me had already firmly, irreversibly, planted its seed.

You have to, as an artist, aim higher than you can reach: that way you may in time extend your range and eventually land further than you thought you could see. And you have to, as a young human, step into the world without care; that way you may in time overcome your fear of becoming yourself.

As I listen to myself on The Tape, I realise I'm listening to a young human who has fearlessly—much more fearlessly than I would ever have imagined myself dare—stepped into the world and is just beginning, just slowly starting, to formulate in it a role for himself now. And this fills me with a new sense of wonder...

Edinburgh

I like Edinburgh. I like it now, I liked it then. I love it now, I loved it then. With one or two reservations, for which Edinburgh is not to blame, nor its good people. It's so far north, it gets undeniably miserable in winter. And dark. The upside of this is that during summer the days are long; and, with its situation by the sea, the light and the air and the atmosphere are tonic.

On The Tape, I refer to it as "a wonderful city," "beautiful," and "absolutely stunning." I also tell my future self that, having queued up at the Fringe Box Office for an hour, and seen people advertise their shows there, "I feel very strongly that next year I will not be here as a member of the audience, but as a participant on some level or other."

My slow delivery and often elaborate choice of words notwithstanding—I really seem to be searching a lot for the exact right way to express myself, and only succeeding maybe seventy, seventy-five percent of the time—I am obviously excited to have discovered "the place to be" for interesting theatre.

I never think of the theatre I had either already done by then, with fellow students in Switzerland, or that I was about to do, in London and Edinburgh with professional actors, as 'avant-garde,' but with hindsight it's also clear to me that much of it probably was.

The theatrical establishment's reluctance or inability to 'get' me as a writer has always baffled me, because nothing I've ever written has ever seemed so 'out there' to me that it could not be both understood and also—if you relish language and appreciate thought as much as emotion, delight in playfulness for its own sake as easily as in losing yourself in a story— enjoyed. Then I read a sentence like the one I've just written, and I think: maybe I do see why some people struggle... (Though in all fairness, that's not how I write most of my dialogue.)

It occurs to me now, and only really now, that with all the wide-eyed wonder and enthusiasm that I started out with, I propelled myself onto a trajectory that is exactly not what then I thought it was going to be. What I remember thinking it was going to be at the time—even though from today's perspective that makes no sense at all—was that I would be heard and seen, ultimately, by everybody, by the general public: I fully assumed that people would, by and by over time, but relatively quickly, become aware of my work, and embrace it. Like it, if you like. And what I find most fascinating now is not that that hasn't happened, that instead some people have certainly loved my plays, but others as absolutely hated them, that not a single one of the new writing theatres has ever put one of them on, even though some have taken pains to invite me into their office, where the Literary Manager would sit me down and profess how impressed they were with what I'd sent them to read but then seem thoroughly perplexed at the idea of doing anything with it; no, what I find most fascinating now is that in spite of all that, and after three decades, I still write work that to me seems entirely 'reasonable,' that is perhaps *individual*, but that certainly does not set out to baffle, and it baffles people.

I don't know this at the time I'm recording my audio diary in August 1988, aged twenty-four, still only three years into living in London, but I'm about to embark on a choppy voyage that will on many occasions have me nearly keel over, that will cause me to get wet a lot, that will have some people so incensed at my work that they will attempt to sink me, but that, yes, will also sail me and my audiences to an island here or a bay there on occasion, where we might make a discovery that we would not otherwise have made, and I know—because sometimes they tell me— that there are indeed those who find value in that.

But perhaps the tone had already been set long before then, when we did *Sentimental*

THE TAPE

Breakdown...—the first of my plays ever to be staged—while I was still at school in Switzerland. One local newspaper had said in its review of the piece, "if it proves anything it is that today's youth has nothing to say." Another found much in it to be encouraged by, and much to encourage. And it's been the same more or less ever since. By and large, I seem to split the critics down the middle, sometimes miles apart from each other, sometimes less so, depending mostly on how conventional or not a piece of writing happens to be. And it would not be long before right here, in Edinburgh, two different reviewers would write about the exact same production that it was "the worst thing" one of them had ever seen, while it was also "the best thing" the other had come across. He wanted, and bought, the T-shirt, he said. I have no reason to doubt either of them. Which is why today, and for some time now, I no longer read 'the reviews': they really are just opinions.

Back then, in August 1988, I tell my future self that Edinburgh is "the place to do something; lively, open, very free, the platform for modern new theatre; and that's me saying this before I have even seen anything." I'm about to see quite a bit: I spend a couple of days at the festival, sleeping little—"it's 34 hours since I've been to bed last, and it's starting to show"—smoking too much, and watching seven shows.

One of these leaves me cold, others I'm quite impressed by, one has me "physically shaking," it's such an "amazing piece of work." I take the opportunity to talk to performers and directors, and to some of the people running the venues to "get some insider views." I see a comedy show which amuses me, but I also tartly remark that "the unfortunate thing is they trap themselves a little; they are very witty, because they parody the Eurovision Song Contest, but their serious songs fall into a category fairly close to the kind they're making jokes about..." but overall I am inspired, encouraged:

"I love Edinburgh," I say in my last entry recorded there. "It is full of beautiful places, full of stunning views; if Edinburgh were blessed enough to find itself located a few degrees further down towards the south, it would be one of the most vibrant and fantastic places to possibly even reside," I venture, using the word 'reside,' still without a hint of irony, I believe, though I express doubts that Edinburgh would have the same atmosphere and cosmopolitan feel outside the festival, and "it's just simply too cold, there's no doubt about that; it feels like April, which is all right for three or four weeks to do some work here, but to live here must be hell, it's so depressing; but funnily enough it doesn't seem to affect the people at all, they are nice and friendly."

And so, even with the cold weather, I am "so invigorated by the people, by what's going on here, by the shows, I could," I say, "go on for a lot longer," but tomorrow I have to check out by 1:30pm, after which I will "then see another three shows at least, and take the eleven-fourteen train from Edinburgh to London, and that will be my festival experience." And even though I still have nearly a third of that experience ahead of me, I'm already able to conclude:

"Only just a couple of months ago, Edinburgh was this colossus of fantastically gifted, possibly famous, experienced, thoroughly professional beings who gathered together, excelling at what they do... – but it's an open space, it's a platform, it's a forum, it's a festival, it's a place where things can be done." I seem to be under no illusion: "The fact that people put in vast amounts of work for what in material terms is no return whatsoever: that creates an environment which to me appears very fruitful." And so the resolution: "If it's the last thing I do, and if it costs me a vast amount of money, I still want to take a show up here."

Thus, I record my own personal manifesto for the following year: "It is now high time, very necessary, very appropriate also, to proceed and do the experiment, see how it works, risk failure, risk loss, risk whatever is involved; and I shall be spending the next twelve months preparing for this experiment and will put it to the test."

And that is, of course, exactly what I then did.

Paris

For many years my most enduring memory of Paris has been this, and I am glad to revisit it, unexpectedly, as I listen to The Tape: I'd arrived at the Gare du Nord at about ten o'clock in the evening on Thursday 18th August, from London.

In London, I had spent "a few hours" at home after returning—aflush, aglow and awonder—from Edinburgh, where the last play I'd seen was an adaptation of Yevgeny Zamyatin's *We*. This had, once more, inspired me, and prompted me to consider whether *QED*, an experimental piece of writing I'd recently conceived essentially as a monologue, "might have a chance in Edinburgh," and I note on The Tape, in a tone that today both amuses and amazes me, that "something at least as good, if not quite a lot better, can be done, actually."

The unencumberedness. The youth. The brazen confidence. The honesty. Now, listening to myself then, I sense I can maybe do what I never could at the time: indulge myself, just a little. Although to others it must have looked and sounded and felt as though everything came incredibly easy to me, it didn't. I never actually indulged myself then: I was, if anything, highly critical of myself and unsure of almost everything. But I tricked myself into appearing otherwise.

Now, I feel a warmth towards me then, a quarter of a century ago, at the beginning, setting out to what is to become me, and I chuckle. I was not a bad person. Perhaps a little deluded (maybe a lot), perhaps a little too sure of myself in some respects, but so very fragile in so many others. And yet, I survived…

I survived because of people like the good human I attach to this memory in Paris. Having arrived at the Gare du Nord at about ten in the evening, I knew I needed to find a train now to Grenoble. Grenoble was really my next stop on this 'Europe Tour 1988,' and try as I might I could not see a train listed to this place anywhere at the Gare du Nord. (It is telling to me now, but not in all seriousness that surprising, that I had not worked out a full itinerary. Taking a train to a European city and from there another train to another city in that same country, without planning or let alone booking a specific connection ahead, to my still European mind was entirely reasonable then.)

THE TAPE

So I walked up to the information desk and in my dodgy French enquired after a train to Grenoble. The lady at the counter talked to me, not unfriendly, but quickly, and made no sense at all. I wandered off and found some other person to start over again, possibly at another information desk or maybe just at the ticket office, and here I fared a little better because while I still was profoundly out of my depth with my inadequate French, I got the gist that in order to get to Grenoble I would first have to go to Lyon, and that while it was not possible at this time of night to catch a train all the way down to Grenoble I could still quite feasibly make it to the station in Lyon.

I must have been travelling on *Interrail* (nowhere on The Tape do I specify) or at any rate have already been in possession of a through ticket to Grenoble, because now, without further purchase, confused but a little relieved, I went searching for said train to Lyon and boarded one which for some reason or other must have looked plausible to me. The train was pretty empty, but it was also pretty late, and I'd done enough grappling with unforeseen complications to give it much thought. Also, I had spent the most part of the last 36 hours on trains, and so I was maybe just a tad tired.

Then suddenly the hum of the air con ceased, and the lights went out. Now fully awake and alert again, I jumped off the train only to see it pull out of the station—all dark, all empty—obviously depot bound. I was stuck, as far as I could tell, at Paris, Gare du Nord, for the night.

Apparently I was not the only one though because a few other lost souls, or travellers

in transit, were lounging about the
concourse around shabby cases or, here
and there, leaning against their backpacks,
and I felt unperturbed, as far as I can recall.

Come midnight or maybe around 1am
they closed the station, and those of us
stranded there with nowhere to go were
moved outside. While some of them
at this point dispersed (they probably
never meant to travel anywhere and were
just seeking shelter inside the station), a
handful or so remained, and I spent the
night talking to a Parisian clochard and
then sleeping next to him a few feet apart
on the pavement outside the Gare du
Nord. When I say 'spent the night,' I mean
really a few night time hours, because at
4:30 they opened the station again, and
those of us who had, or thought we had,
trains to catch were let back inside.

Now, what on The Tape in my a little self-conscious and just slightly off-the-mark English I refer to as "sufficiently tired" (having spent the second night in a row getting all of about two hours sleep), I walk up to the ticket office as soon as it opens and make my third attempt at establishing how to get to Grenoble from Paris.

I finally find out that in order to get to Grenoble from Paris I first have to go to the Gare de Lyon. Not the Gare de Lyon in Lyon, where you would expect it to be, but the Gare de Lyon in Paris. Suddenly a lot of bizarre and circuitous conversation the night before begins to make sense: they were talking about the railway station in Paris called Lyon, and I was understanding the railway station of Lyon, all the time.

THE TAPE

To get to the Gare de Lyon in Paris, I'm informed, I can take either the *métro* or a *banlieu* train. And so, after asking a few more people, I find myself in front of this gigantic ticket machine that looks to me like the unsolvable puzzle, like a mysterious lock to which no key can be known, like an impenetrable riddle in an unbreakable code.

By this time I can barely keep my eyes open, and even if I do: I've taken out my contact lenses for the few hours' rest on the pavement outside, and my glasses are somewhere at the bottom of my bag. I stand there like Ali Baba having forgotten the magical phrase for Sesame, when a chap pitches up, charming and bright eyed, and asks me if I'm lost.

'Not really...' I say, which now strikes me as disingenuous, and I tell him I just need to get to the Gare de Lyon. He asks me if I'm from London. 'Yes,' I say, and give him a weary smile. He tells me that a friend of his had been to London for three days, and keys in the correct sequence. I'm trying to process if that was just recently that his friend had been to London for three days, or once in his lifetime, and what the further significance of this may be, but the price flashes up on the machine, and it now dawns on me that I haven't got any francs yet. Before I can explain, he throws in some coins and hands me the ticket and wishes me good luck. I barely manage a 'thank you' before he is gone, vanished into the early commuter throng of Parisians.

I have never forgotten this man and his random act of kindness. He changed not only the way I thought about 'the people of Paris' (they had a fearsome reputation), but completely opened my eyes to what a

small deed could do; and because I was so
grateful and so touched and so genuinely
helped out by what he had done for me,
I often and in many situations since have
tried to emulate his disposition towards me
and pass on the love. And I still do, three
decades later.

And so if anything I ever was able to do
for a 'stranger' has had even a fraction
of the impact he had on me, then this
young man—with a smile, two minutes of
his time, and what must have amounted
to about three or four francs of his
money—has made the world a much,
much better place.

Merci, mon ami. Tu es toujours dans mon âme...

Songs & Charades

I take the "fabulous" TGV to Lyon—from said Gare de Lyon, there now safely and without further trouble arrived—and change to another, ordinary train to Grenoble where I get to Anne's at 1pm and meet "the others."

The others are certainly Magda, my flatmate from London, whose friend Anne is, and Magda's dancer friend Ross, who, like her, is from Glasgow, and whom I have met on one or two occasions before, fancying him ever so slightly, but getting from him principally polite indifference, which doesn't trouble me more than to about that same level: just ever so slightly.

There may have been other 'others,' but I wouldn't be certain now who, and The

THE TAPE

Tape here doesn't elaborate, so maybe there weren't.

What The Tape does tell me is that I now experience a "wonderful sequence of days." I have virtually no recollection of this. But according to myself, we spend the afternoon playing charades (this sounds entirely plausible, knowing Magda), and in the evening we hook up with some friends of Anne's.

In my still and always a tad cautious, somewhat incongruous English, I describe this as "so enjoyable, so nice," as we go out "for a meal" and have "lots to eat, lots to drink." Then, after dinner and drinks, we get back home to Anne's and sing songs. We go to bed "very late, at 4 in the morning, or so." I can imagine this, vividly enough, but not remember.

I do remember what comes next, a bit: it's a very slow, very lazy, relaxing Saturday. (In my memory, it's a Sunday, but that hardly matters...) The weather is "very cold," and it's raining, which is a good excuse to stay indoors, I record (though this bit again I no longer remember), and play more charades. What I do remember is doing (or helping with) some washing up, and looking out of the window into the cold grey weekend and feeling properly chuffed.

That glow of contentment, a little hungover, I remember it well. (Only now it occurs to me that that was another occasion entirely: that was Glasgow, where we spent Hogmanay one year, possibly the same year, with essentially the same people, Magda and Ross, and quite possibly also Anne. The blurring of the past in the mind over time...)

In the evening, more people come around, and we sing more songs, play the guitar, drink a lot; and by the time I actually record my next entry, it's Sunday, "a couple of extremely pleasant days" having passed.

Sunday I also have an actual recollection of. The weather had turned fine again, and we took guitars (I imagine there were at least two) out to a little pond, where we all of us sat on the jetty and sang songs in the sun. This, really, is the second enduring memory I have of the whole trip, after the friendly Parisian coming to my rescue: it's a hazy memory, and in my mind it looks exactly like the kind of 1970s or 80s film where, to tell the audience that something is being remembered, the picture goes all diffuse and vastly overexposed: it's a warm, light, comfortable glow, just not very clear, not at all distinct. Then again, it doesn't have to be.

I've just told The Tape that Magda and Ross are going to continue their journey tonight (where to I don't say and don't remember), whereas I will stay on for another day and then continue my trip to Italy.

Magda walks in on me—possibly having heard me talk 'to myself,' which in an age before mobiles is not the usual thing for someone to do—and, with that mix of curiosity and concern in her voice that makes it go a little high pitched, asks me what I'm doing. I explain to her that I'm recording an audio diary, and that I'll be able to play it to her at some point, though I don't think I ever did play it to her. I don't think I ever played it to anyone, and now that I'm listening to it, for the first time in twenty-eight years, I keep getting that sense of near sacred wonder. Songs and charades. Songs and charades...

It was a blissful time. I know it was because although I have hardly any recollection of it, I have a recording of me talking about it. I'm not effusive in my joy, but I know I'm living through another best time of my life.

The first one, surely, was at the Gymnasium Münchenstein, where I spent one and a half years in near comprehensive, intensive, fully lived happiness. Because of the people I was at school with, because of the projects we were doing (we performed my first play and took it on a mini tour to Zürich and a place called Liestal, and it was a tremendous success with the audiences wherever we went), because of the discoveries, the newness of it all. Pain too, yes, now and then, but not much and not lasting and not beyond what you'd expect in your final years of growing up.

The classic freedom of not having any responsibilities yet at all, but being able to follow your inclinations. To travel, to drive (on a whim to Munich and back in a couple of days, with a girl friend who was then almost my girlfriend), to experiment, to be cool. To make a statement and feel good about it. I'm certain we knew then that we were happy and privileged and hopeful and young; and we still knew it, almost as much, in Grenoble, that weekend in August of 1988. The notion I keep coming back to: unencumbered. At ease, with ourselves, with it all.

I'm glad now I have this Tape. I shall keep it, of course, and—if I'm around and still have a machine to play it then—listen to it again in another twenty-five years or so. I have a feeling it will sound no different. It's endearing, to me at least, to hear me like this, but it is so remote. So unrecognisable: I'm listening to the stories of a young man I barely know at all. How strange. How fascinating too, but how odd. To not, more deeply, feel connected. As someone who thinks connection is everything and that everything *is* in fact connected...

Towards Italy

Tuesday I travel on, taking an early morning train that departs at 7:21, towards Italy. The journey, The Tape tells me, is "fairly pleasant," with the exception of one incident. This sits ingrained on my brain, and whilst most of the other experiences of that August are a haze with only the occasional moment or image in any kind of focus, this one is sharp and clear, and it still makes me squirm, to this day.

I was tired. I had slept for two hours, again... – Monday night we'd decided to go to the cinema: Anne and some of her friends had gone to see some American movie I evidently did not rate or care about, and I had gone to see *Le Grand Bleu:* "one of the most stunningly beautiful

THE TAPE

films I've ever seen," I now hear myself rave, and I remember that vividly too, though not only from this screening, but from another, much more thrilling one, later, in Paris. Jean-Marc Barr. "He is fantastic; he's certainly a name to remember." After the cinema, a crepe, and then to bed really late.

So, with very little sleep, I'm on a train that is completely full, though I do have a seat, by the window, near the end of the carriage. I mostly daydream and possibly doze off a bit now and then, and everything is going fine until the train stops at a spot where there seems to be nothing at all. It's not a town, it's not a village. It's barely a hamlet. There's a platform and a small building, and there are some signs that to me in my state, which is not comatose but not alert either, are meaningless.

On board come two customs officers.
I see them appear at the other end of
the carriage, quite far away from where
I am, and as I look up at them, I semi-
consciously give a sigh of profoundest
ennui, just exactly at the moment that one
of them catches my eye.

I think nothing more of this for the next
five minutes or so and continue gazing out
of the window, thinking my nondescript
thoughts. My sigh and my facial expression
had lasted for maybe a second. But I do
remember distinctly allowing that gut
response to just come out: an aversion to
officialdom. Almost, but almost not quite,
wanting to show them I held them in a
sizeable degree of post-juvenile contempt,
not as human beings, of course, but as
uniforms holding up the train's so effortless
glide through the artificially delineate
countryside.

THE TAPE

The two officials make their way through the carriage, checking passports, not hassling anyone. They work quite fast, and I'm almost beginning to like them for being so efficient and quick about their monotonous task. Then they get to me. I am sitting by my window, resting my head on my hand, and I look up at them, extremely tired and bored. I am wearing all black. I am twenty-four, with peroxide dyed hair. I had reacted to spotting them from a distance with a look on my face and body language that to them must have signalled not so much *ennui* as 'trouble.' I am their prime suspect. Certainly of the carriage, probably of the train. Possibly of the day, maybe the month.

Granted, it could have been worse. They could have taken me off the train and subjected me to a strip search. They didn't.

They went through everything I had on me. They opened my luggage (I seem to recall this being a big holdall bag), searched through my clothes, opened my toiletry bag.

They found a tiny tube of something and demanded to know what it was. It was a cream for mosquito bites. They thought that hard to believe, which was ridiculous, because it was clearly labelled, smelt like medicine, and we were on the border to Italy, in the summer. My brain was not willing to argue. My Italian register brought forth: *zanzare*.

It took about twenty minutes, it felt like two hours. It was not even humiliating so much as it was unnecessary and, I felt, vindictive. This, I now know, is what profiling feels like, if you match the profile. This is what being exposed to low-level

THE TAPE

authority feels like if it turns against you. Today, I understand people who complain about stop-and-search policies, or who are tired of being the ones picked out at airport entry points because of their skin tone or what they are wearing. It was, by comparison, harmless, and yet I wanted it just to end. I felt exposed and hard done by. And I was.

Still. I had never in my life purchased or carried any illegal substance, and so I had nothing on me, and they did not find anything. They left, we departed, I arrived in Milan, where I did something really stupid.

I got off the train and went into the station to look at the board where all the trains were displayed. Vicenza, this told me, would next be up at 2pm. It was now getting towards half one, but, for some to me now unfathomable reason not trusting that intelligence, I decided to go to the information desk to make sure. There was only one window open: *'Money Exchange & Information.'* After queueing for half an hour, I arrived at said window, only to find that this was the wrong one. Nonetheless, they asked me what I wanted to know, and I told them I wanted to know when the next train would leave for Vicenza. At 2pm they said, glancing idly at a timetable. I ran, as best I could with my bag, to the platform, where I saw the train pull out of the station. What, I wonder, was that all about? Sometimes I just didn't trust myself. At all.

I phoned my friend Stefano in Vicenza from a public phone box, which cost me 600 lire, I record, to tell him I'd be arriving one hour later. Stefano, once I'd got there and had settled, took me to the beautiful piazza in the town centre, where we also met up with our mutual friend Giovanni.

Thus begins about a week in Vicenza, and at the hands of Stefano's mum, I tell The Tape, I'm being fed to the point of bursting.

I spend one day in Venice, mostly at the Peggy Guggenheim Collection, and, passing one of the many small shops, I see a leather jacket I particularly like the look of. I go inside and casually ask the shop assistant how much it costs (there being no price tag). Five million lire, she tells me, which at the time is about two thousand pounds. 'I see,' I say, as matter of factly (or so I think) as I can, and I do this unnecessary thing of looking at it in a little more detail to signal that I'm really not perturbed at all by the price. I'm really perturbed by the price. Then I do that even

more unnecessary thing of looking around
the shop a bit further before I leave, just to
make sure the middle-aged woman whom
I will never meet again in my life, and who
has long since sussed that I'm in the wrong
shop, understands that the prices here are
really no big deal for me, at all. They're a
really big deal for me…

Vicenza, I tell my self of the future, is
incredibly quiet, but I like the Teatro
Olympico, calling it "stunning." Built like
a Greek arena, but all indoors, I describe it
as "absolutely beautiful" and venture that
it may be the only one of its kind in Italy
(though where I get that from, or whether
it is true, I don't know).

At one point we go to a party together,
which I confide to The Tape reminds me
of the time when we, I and my *gschpänlis*
from the Gymnasium Münchenstein, had

our parties: the ease, the freedom. I feel charmed, I put on record, and delighted by the friendliness of these people.

I also go back to Venice on "various occasions" (there can't have been many, considering how long I was in Vicenza for), and on one of these get to see a Pier Paolo Pasolini film at the festival, apparently as a matter of extreme luck: "How I managed to get there and get there on time, I will never know, but it worked, and it worked to the minute." I seem to have walked into some post office (presumably having got to the Lido first), and asked where the auditorium was that I needed to get to, only to find that it just so happened to be that particular building, where the film was about to start. What exactly the film was I don't put on record...

There are two more moments that stick in my memory from Vicenza, and although I don't talk about them on The Tape, I am as certain as I can be that they belong to that same trip. (I've since been back to Vicenza a number of times, and there was most likely at least one more visit within the next year or two, but the way things fit together—especially with the amount of time I seem to have on my own whilst staying with Stefano and his family, who are presumably out working—makes me think that this is all one occasion.)

The first one involved me attempting to make coffee with one of these typical two-part Italian coffee jugs. I took the thing, which I myself had just used and which was still hot, off the hob and, wearing oven gloves, unscrewed the top from the bottom. At that point there was an almighty bang, and ground coffee splattered all over the immaculately clean small town kitchen, covering every available surface in fine specks of wet brown sediment. Stefano was grace personified and just helped me clean up before his mum got back home…

The other one takes place in Vicenza town. I go up to a small church that is either closed or about to close and there's a young, good-looking guard at the gate. This makes me think it might have been a small museum or some other historic site, since churches didn't usually have guards, as far as I can remember. He wears a uniform of the nondescript charcoal or dark grey variety, and to my surprise he opens the door for me and shows me around.

We get to the end of a short tour at the lowest part of the building, a crypt or a vault, of which I do not recall what it contained, and there is this moment that stays in my mind. This moment when something is meant to happen. And nothing happens. I wasn't sure then what it was that was meant to happen, and I'm not even entirely sure today.

Looking back I wonder: was he about to make a move on me? If so, why didn't he? I was, then, I now see, quite attractive, though I didn't think so then. We were alone. He had keys to the building, he had, most probably, locked the front door. I liked him. I think I would have wanted him to make a move. I certainly wouldn't have made a move first, though. I was on foreign territory, I was far too shy and too gauche, and also nowhere near conceited enough: I never assumed people fancied me so much as to want to make a move on me; sometimes until long after they did. Maybe I was too aloof too.

With hindsight maybe I understand why
he might not have made a move, even if he
had wanted to and had felt that I possibly
wanted him to, and the conditions were
well nigh perfect for, well, at least a kiss,
just to see how that would feel and where
it would lead. I had a barrier up, then,
practically always; I was not just aloof, but
also distant, remote. What a pity…

The moment lasted—not very long—until
it was over, and he led me back upstairs
into the Italian sunshine. I thanked
him, I said goodbye. And I wondered:
what was that? Did I miss something
here? This feeling, this question: did
I just miss something here, that was
happening, or should have been happening,
or could have been happening, if only I'd
been alert to it, perhaps less naive, perhaps
less insecure, perhaps more attuned:

it followed me for years, for decades even. Until recently. It doesn't do so much any more: I miss things occasionally, still, but not quite so much as a rule. And I make mistakes, of course, who doesn't. And sometimes I'm just not brave enough. In fact, I often, I think, am probably just not quite brave enough.

And then on the way onwards, in Milan, I actually went to some nondescript building in the outskirts of somewhere and tried to talk to somebody from the Italian TV network *Reteitalia*. What on earth about, I have no idea...

Helvetia

From Milan I take the train to Chur. Chur has never been my favourite place in the world, and it's not difficult for me to say why: it feels dour. It is, apparently, the oldest city in Switzerland, and it has, I believe, several things going for it, none of which is entirely evident to me. Mainly because it sits hemmed in by big mountains that deprive it of light, almost completely, in winter, while not being splendid enough in the summer to offer any type of gorgeousness in terms of a view. My sister at this time lives in Chur, and I am heading towards her to spend a couple of days with her, The Tape tells me.

My memory of this is, again, hazy, but I'm clearly delighted: "It is wonderful," I narrate, "to spend time together and talk," for the first time in years. And I know this was so. To this day, I enjoy spending time with my sister, though to this day I don't do so often enough, and on this occasion, we must have had a lot to say to each other: I was back in the country where I grew up, but which I had always struggled and never found it either necessary or entirely possible to call home, for the first time since, almost exactly three years earlier, I had left with two suitcases, one red and one black (and neither of them with castors) and a friend's address in my pocket, in Enfield, thence to make London my home.

Helvetia. I like thinking of Switzerland as Helvetia. It has something sturdy, Celtic, dependable to it. Unique. Firm and reassuring. 'Switzerland' sounds—maybe because it so much has become—like a brand, a theme park, a place where you go on holiday. Helvetia is a place you

were rooted in, once. Whether you then
uprooted yourself, and for whatever
reasons, fades into the background, into
the fabric: it does not become insignificant
(nothing of that kind ever does), but it's
just there, part of the character, part of
the being, part of the history, part of the
substance, the core. And so is Helvetia.

The train from Milan to Chur, I relate
to The Tape, "took absolutely ages," but
also "provided the most admirable views."
It's one of these instances where I betray
the fact that I'm still not on top of the
subtleties of the English language. I hear
myself do that a lot on this recording: I
nearly get the word right, but not quite. I
still, from the back of my mind, translate
traces from German, maybe not so much
words, as concepts, perhaps. I'm just not
quite there, yet.

THE TAPE

In Treviso I change trains and board "this incredible little red train, consisting of about three carriages, all the way up, over the San Bernardino Pass." Here my memory suddenly kicks in again, vivid and strong.

I remember this journey, this train. And with awe. I remember the windows being open and the warm summer air wafting in; I remember the noise, intermittently suddenly so much louder, going through tunnels; I remember the green and red covered seats: red for smoking, green for non. I was a smoker then, I may have been travelling red. Then again, I may already have been doing what I used to do for a while: park myself in the non-smoking section and nip to the red part of the carriage for the occasional cigarette. The train wasn't full, I remember it being almost empty. It's a glorious journey, and one you can still do. Now, they have state-of-the-art rolling stock with huge panorama windows, and smoking is a definite no-no, but the trains are no faster, and the views no less stunning, than they were then.

I seem to also recall that I met up here with an old school friend whom I would shortly be linking up with again in Paris, but The Tape makes no mention of this, so perhaps I am wrong. Come the following Saturday, I take a train to Basel.

This is where I went to school, this is where I grew up: the first twenty-one years of my life. I spend eight or nine hours talking to Peggy, my best friend then and my best friend now from our high school days, and today as then, when we meet, we find ourselves talking for hours. Eight or nine is nothing unusual: if you pitch up at six, have an *apéro,* have dinner, sit out on the balcony, keep on talking, before you know it, it's three in the morning...

On Sunday Peggy, my mum and I go to see an exhibition (I don't tell The Tape which one, and I can't remember), and then my brother comes round with his two sons, one of whom is my godson. There is a photograph of this occasion, which takes place in my parents' garden, with me sitting between the two boys, looking at a picture book, maybe reading them the story. My mother, a little while later, sent me this picture in a card with a quote in German: *Es ist ein ungeheures Glück wenn man fähig ist, sich freuen zu können.* German websites attribute this to George Bernard Shaw. I try to find the English original, and so far I fail. 'It is a tremendous fortune to be able to find joy in things,' is more or less how I would translate it back, but it still sounds more clunky than it should. If it's Shaw. Maybe it's been misattributed, that's possible: many things are.

"Then we went to see *Ironweed* at the cinema." I don't remember anything about this, the film or who is 'we' in this instance, but my 24-year-old self puts on record that "it was like no time had passed at all." Maybe because hardly any time had passed, a mere three years…

Tuesday I spent in Zürich, "meeting, luckily, Benjamin for the first time in absolutely years," and also Beatrice. Benjamin. Beatrice. These two people: they are lodged in my mind, in my soul. Benjamin more than Beatrice, and in a much different way, but both register, both matter, both shaped who I was and therefore who I now am.

THE TAPE

The meeting with Benjamin I remember clearly. He was his usual, laconic self. He was the boy I was most in love with, for a very long time. We were in no relationship, he never, as far as I know, reciprocated my feelings, he was not even gay, he was just the boy I most loved.

By this time, he would have been about twenty-two, and he'd either just been released or was on day-release from prison. He'd been sentenced to prison for no crime: he was a conscientious objector and had refused to do military service, which in Switzerland at the time carried a prison term and a criminal record. He was unfazed by his time in prison: he took this, as he seemed to take everything, in his stride. Granted, the way he talked about it, it also sounded like prison for conscientious objectors in Switzerland was by now a gentle affair.

He was beautiful, as I had always seen
him, and unruffled. Unexcitable, but good
humoured. I'd carried him around in my
heart for the entire duration I'd been living
in London, and I continued to do so for
many years after. It was only really when
one day, on a Sunday afternoon, he phoned
me, out of the blue, to tell me he'd received
a letter I had sent him many months earlier,
care of his mother, and we talked for maybe
five hours or so on the phone, both getting
increasingly woozy on our respective
drinks, that I was able to put that love
where it belonged: in the past, in my youth.
In a time before even our reunion here now
in Zürich.

I have memories of us sitting at my parents'
home next to each other on the sofa
all night long talking, drinking coffee,
almost getting high on it, so much of it we

drank; of us walking in the fields near his parents' home on Lake Zürich on a wintry afternoon; of us first meeting at a school fete... I have everything with me still, as if it were yesterday. But only since maybe ten years ago, slightly less, am I able to think of it really as yesterday. I believe I once kissed him, I'm not even sure. I'm sure that I always wanted to. Always.

How deeply that boy had seeped into the folds of my brain. How strongly he clasped my heart; how warmly, how tenderly I longed for him, for how long. I still have his letters, of course. I no longer have this desire: I'm glad it has gone, I was able to bid it farewell. Not the memory though, not the fondness. I am over him now, but I cannot, and nor do I need to, get over how much I loved him.

Beatrice, I also remember, also fondly, but not on that day. I certainly kissed her, and she me. She was, I'm quite certain, keener on me than I was on her, but I liked her, and for a short while it was as if we were together. How strange, to think of it now. But that alone, having been the girl with whom I was once almost together, secures her a place in my self. She, too, is part of me; was then, is now.

Wednesday a lunch with a friend. "In all," I recount on The Tape, I "had a chance to see lots of people." Also my grandfather. I was "very worried about grandfather, he looked very ill and weak; he was very nice, but I have an impression that any time we meet might be the last time." And so, I believe, it proved, on this occasion.

{Bereavement}

This is not on The Tape, but I'm reminded of it here, and part of me thinks it doesn't belong here, part of me thinks it doesn't belong anywhere really, part of me wonders does everything somehow, ultimately, need to be told, and part of me knows: this is exactly where it belongs.

I hear myself overall so happy, so optimistic on The Tape. Improbably casual and emotionally understated: my delivery suggests I'm giving an account of a trip to Milton Keynes, but the words I choose—carefully, even cautiously, deliberately always—speak of a young person with everything going for himself, with abundance of confidence, and imbued with great hope. And I'm so glad to hear him thus, though in the tone of the voice and the distance to the heart, I also hear the youth from which this young person had emerged, then relatively recently.

I've been blessed in that I have, to this day, had to suffer the loss of three people only. And of a cat. Of these three, one was someone I'd met once, very briefly, but really didn't know: Diana, the Princess of Wales. There is no rhyme or reason to this, but her death shook me to the core and disorientated me for a week. I cried more over her than any of my grandparents, all of whom I loved dearly. All my grandparents died over the years, but that seemed the normal course of the world: people get old, then they die. Obviously, their passing was, in each case, a loss, and felt as one, too. But you can prepare for this, you know it's going to happen, and when it does, you deal with it, and then you honour them in your thoughts and keep their memory alive in your soul. Princess Diana being torn out of our culture was a cataclysm. Of its own kind. It came out of nowhere, and it seemed to change everything, and, irrational though this was, it left a gaping hole in my life, in a way that I, myself, never expected. It was an extraordinary experience, unique, I am certain, to her.

One was a dear friend who decided to leave us. That was both shocking and unexpected, even if it had been, in a way, predictable, sadly. I mourned her, and I knew then, as I know now, that I had to let that be as it was. It was just so. More than anything I felt I was called upon to respect her, and her decision. And that's what I did, and that's what I do.

Losing our cat as a boy was dreadful: I loved that cat. I was unspeakably sad when we were told he'd been hit by the tram. I got over it.

And one is still around and still a good friend, and when we see each other now we have excellent conversations, but when I first lost him—I was fifteen, he fourteen—my world fell apart. We had been best friends at school, and we were in essence together. Not as lovers, not romantically, not anything other than as friends, but as friends we were as one. People didn't even tease us, it was just the accepted thing, that where I was there was he, and where he was was I.

It had come about over several years, and it was my normality. Of course I loved him, but I didn't know that. I had no conception of love (and none of sexuality, for that matter), I spent no time thinking about how much I needed him, or enjoyed being

{BEREAVEMENT}

with him, or relied on him always being
around. That was all just the way it was. It
was solid, it was dependable, it was real.

And then something happened that
I hadn't seen coming, ever: he turned
away from me. It was gradual, simple,
undramatic, and also in its own way
normal: he just started spending time with
someone else, more than with me. At first I
barely noticed, there was no cut-off point,
no moment I could pinpoint where it
began, it just gradually dawned on me: we
are no longer one.

The other boy was a good person, still
is: we're still friends as well, he and I.
He wasn't cruel, he didn't manoeuvre,
or manipulate, he just took my place,
without, probably, even knowing what was
happening, either. I had been the one who
was always by my friend's side, and now

he was there. At first he was there too, but soon he was there more than I, and then I realised I had lost my love. I still couldn't name it that, because I still didn't know that that's what it was, but the incision was brutal. I was cut off. I bled.

I was lost. Abandoned. Bereaved. I couldn't name the way I felt any of these things, because I didn't know what they were, I only knew that I didn't want to live. Really didn't. Not melodramatically, attention seekingly didn't, just didn't. There was no point. I was distraught, yes, but more than that I was destroyed. There was no word for it, no expression, no therapy and no remedy, there was just emptiness, complete.

This lasted for eighteen months, maybe twenty. It was a crisis so profound, so categorical, so total, I felt that it would break me. I saw no way that it couldn't.

{BEREAVEMENT}

It was absolute, the despair. And all of this over the loss of a *friend*? Today, with perspective, I know it was obviously more than that: losing my friend was the trigger. What his extracting himself from my life did was tear open a wound which drew all manner of complications. The insecurity. The loneliness. The mind's confusion over the heart. The heartbreak over the part of the soul that was missing. The pointlessness. The disorientation.

What sustained me was my brother, because I could talk to him—not about this, but about everything else that was going on in my teenage life—and my mother of course, because I could not then, and I would not now be able to, bring myself to do anything deliberately that would cause her grief.

THE TAPE

And then something happened that I also didn't expect: I found a way out. I hadn't been looking, not consciously anyway, I wouldn't have known where to start, but the subconscious knows and searches and finds, and without thinking much what I was doing, I wrote.

It was going to be and started out briefly as a novel, but then I remembered something our English teacher had said: that writing plays is way more efficient than writing novels: you need far fewer words to tell your story and to create your characters.

And so I wrote my first play. I was seventeen now, I called it *19*. It dealt with a young man taking his life, and how that affects everyone around him. It had an original structure, because rather than going in a linear plot from beginning through middle to end, it started with events about a year or two (I can't remember exactly) before and after the suicide and then circled in, closer and closer, to end with the moment of no return. That structure, too, was not something I really thought about, I just wrote it that way. Although the play has never been performed, nor ever even been read in public, it achieved several things for me.

Firstly, it was my catharsis. By abstracting the youth's self-inflicted death and putting it on a character in a play, I was able to 'deal with' what I was going through, and absolved myself from actually having to do the same thing for real.

Secondly, it showed me I had a new friend. I gave this piece—which was really very revelatory, open and incredibly honest—to somebody I had started spending time with at school, and his reaction was perfect: he took it seriously, but he didn't panic. He just talked about it as a piece of writing, and encouraged me to show it to other people, which I did. I knew now I had someone again I could trust.

Thirdly, it made me realise I was able to write. I gave the piece to my German teacher at school who, unbeknownst to me, gave it to a man who happened to be my favourite actor at the Stadttheater Basel, where we routinely saw maybe a dozen plays each season. Henning Köhler. He was invited to our school to give a talk about theatre and acting generally, and at the end of that talk he said: "and one of you has written a really good play." I went up to him afterwards and said: "that may have been me."

Nothing happened with or to the play, he was quite apologetic about that—'I'm really sorry, I can't do anything for you in terms of getting it on at the theatre'—but for Henning Köhler, to my mind the best actor in town, to have read my play and to have made a point of mentioning it, that was enough. That was something I could hold on to.

And it also paved the way for me to lose my virginity, at last. There was a man whom I knew well and liked and respected a lot, a writer, actor, performer, who lived in St Gallen, of all places, and I sent him the play. I knew he was gay, he was a few years older than me, in his early twenties. He was cool. And nice. And in an unspectacular way attractive.

He read the play and asked me if I wanted to come and talk about it, and I said yes. I went to visit him, and we talked about the play, and at the end of the evening, I went to sleep on the sofa, and he came over and said: "If you want to you can come to my bed?" And I said, "yes."

The doors were finally flung open. It wasn't quite the proverbial floodgates, though in a Hollywood rendering of the story there would probably have to be strings; but it was good. I was happy. I'd pulled through.

And I knew then, and I've known ever since, that having coped with that period of my life, and survived it, I'd be able to cope with anything. That was one great big case of something that could have killed me, but didn't, and so made me stronger. A lot.

My enduring memory of this handsome man is on stage. He was singing a version of *Es liegt was in der Luft*—'there's something in the air'—to which he had written new lyrics. He'd turned it into a satirical number, as part of an environmental cabaret revue. It was glorious. And a roaring success. He was so alive, so in it, so buoyed by the love from the audience, so overjoyed about doing this, and doing it well.

Many years later—not on this trip, another eight years or so after that—I was in Basel where I'd heard he had since taken on a job as Artistic Director of a small theatre.

It was a sunny afternoon, and I walked into the foyer, to see if he happened to be around, just to say hello, on a whim. I asked a young man who was doing something to the display. "Oh," he said. And I can still see the look on his face, of surprise and regret: "No. I'm sorry. He died a few months ago."

THE TAPE

I salute you, my friend, and I thank you for the time, the patience, the generosity and the inspiration: you genuinely helped me find my way – your spirit lives.

Les Grands Amours

I arrive back in Paris, and see it "properly" now "for the first time." These mark the "last few days of a fantastic holiday," and "those few days were wonderful."

I feel that glow now, it expands beneath my ribs and makes my breath seem warmer. "I think my favourite building in the world for its originality is the Centre Pompidou," I tell myself on The Tape, and for a long time, I remember, that was the case. I embraced modernity, pre-, post- and present. I was *into* things, such as cool architecture; they excited me then, they excite me still.

I record and recall seeing *La Vie de Brian*, as *The Life of Brian* was called there, and us laughing our heads off, the way we only could then. There was an evening, not long after I'd moved to London, when my friend Peggy and, I believe, beautiful Stefan, and maybe one or two other people were assembled in my shared living room, lounging on the grubby sofa and draped over a stained but strangely comfortable armchair, watching *Airplane!* on TV. We laughed so hard at this, we literally ended up on the floor. That capacity for joy, so unalloyed: we had it then, we had it in Paris—that was exactly the era—and I don't know when or where it went. That freshness, even with an open mind as I try to keep it, has simply gone: hardly anything ever makes me laugh now anywhere near as hard. Perhaps I've seen it, heard it, if not all then just too much of it, to tickle me so with surprise?

I remember loving the Pompidou, I remember loving and laughing at *La Vie*,

I remember little if anything else, apart from Christian, Judith's brother, whom I thought "great" and "quite eccentric, in his own way," and probably fancied, just a bit. Judith, whom I loved then and still love today, though I haven't seen her in a decade (and then under sad, troubled, circumstances concerning our friend), was my school pal whom we were visiting in Paris, where she was staying with her boyfriend, Alain. For reasons I don't recall I spent quite some time with her brother, liking him immensely. (Maybe because Judith was with her boyfriend, Alain?)

At one point Christian and I got on a metro train together. As it arrived, we noticed that it had first and second class compartments, and he said we should ride in second class since we didn't have first class tickets. I, having never been to Paris "properly" before, convinced him that this must be a remnant of the olden days, and that by now the metro surely only had one class for all. So we boarded the less crowded first class carriage.

Within minutes we were surrounded by about five ticket inspectors, demanding a surcharge and a fine. I was outraged: I told them they were being completely unreasonable, since it was impossible for me, a Londoner, to know that a metropolitan underground train could have two classes. They pointed at the big '1' that was painted on the interior of the carriage, and mentioned the same on the outside. I was having none of it: I live in London, I said, I use the tube all the time, and we don't have any of this nonsense. They let us off. We were made to move to second class, but no money changed hands. I can be stubborn when I need to be, that hasn't changed...

My forever enduring memory though of these last few days of my Europe tour in 1988, and one of the best and most cherished experiences of all my years of going to the cinema anywhere in the world, was *Le Grand Bleu.* I had seen it before, in Grenoble, and fallen in love with it and with Jean-Marc Barr then, but this now was in a league of its own.

The film was immensely successful in France, and so *Le Grand Rex,* one of the largest cinemas in Paris, had put up an extra large screen in front of its existing one. It was, I tell The Tape, "a 25 metre screen," which would make it either nearly the size of, or even slightly bigger than, the screen on the Piazza Grande at the Locarno Film Festival (which today is still the largest in Europe), depending on whether that was a horizontal width or a diagonal

measurement, which I can't remember.
In any case, it was huge. (They may even
have 'renamed' the cinema for that run. It's
entirely possible, but once again I am no
longer certain, that the cinema was really
normally called *Le Rex,* and they labelled it
Le Grand Rex just for *Le Grand Bleu,* with
the big screen.)

Because the screen was so large, there were
now, in the auditorium, new restricted
sight lines. The stalls were fine, as was the
upper balcony, but from all but the front
row in the dress circle, the view was severely
restricted, because you would not see the
top of the screen (which was blocked off
by the balcony above you) or the bottom
(which was obscured by the circle in front
of you), for which reason the cinema had
cordoned off the dress circle altogether.

We were not young people to be told where to sit in a cinema with unreserved seating, and so while people raced, as the doors opened, to the best seats up on the balcony and down in the stalls, we opened the door to the dress circle behind the red cord, and saw it empty, with a vast screen beckoning. We snuck in, closed the door behind us, and took up the few seats in the centre of the front row of the dress circle, the ones directly in the middle of the screen: your entire field of vision was taken up with *The Big Blue:* it was *magnificent*.

I to this day can't get over how beautiful and real the sea and how close-enough-to-touch Jean-Marc Barr were. Other good actors appeared in the film, there was other fine scenery, but I remember him and the sea and the dolphins. And the party on Taormina, I believe, where he turns up dressed in a dinner suit, wearing trainers, looking sheepish and unbearably cute. I could have married him there and then.

I later met Jean-Marc Barr after a performance in the West End of a Tennessee Williams play, and he was gracious and polite; I a little timid and shy, but happy to be face-to-face with him in person, and now getting him 'out of my system': he was a lovely, good-looking man, and a very decent actor, and I no longer now had to pine...

"Unfortunately, on the last night" of our stay in Paris, I tell The Tape, "Judith split up with her boyfriend, Alain," and so "went back with her brother Christian," to Basel, I presume. I, on Sunday, which therefore must have been the next day, took the train back to London and arrived there in the evening, "about nine o'clock."

London

The Tape ends in London, where I tell my future self that I had "never been on a holiday after which I found it so difficult to return home."

It was my longest trip since leaving high school in Switzerland, after which eleven of us had gone island hopping in Greece for nearly a month. I don't feel like coming "back to my own cooking"—which at the time, and for many, many years to come, consists mainly of pasta, fried eggs and the occasional oven-baked fish—"and my own washing up." The only thing I do feel like is to "bring to fruition all the plans I've formulated about Edinburgh."

It feels good to have "talked to so many people in so many different places;" in fact, "it feels like there's a theatre, and friends and family are already assembled in the front rows, but the curtain hasn't quite risen yet." But that's good, I emphasise: "it's a kind of pressure—good pressure—a supportive expectation, which spurs me on to follow through on what I said I wanted to do." Of course, I am aware, "I don't know if it will succeed, but it's worth a try." And for that sentiment alone I today salute my very young and very optimistic self of 1988.

A few changes are imminent: "I feel I have to leave 14 St Alban's Street soon, just because of the temperatures in winter." These I remember with less pain now than I know I used to experience at the time. The place had no central heating, and while the kitchen (which was also the hall) and my bedroom were so small that you could just about get them warm with an

electric blow heater or by putting on the
oven and leaving its door open, that was
an expensive and hardly ecological way to
heat your home, and we all had no money.
So in winter, we took all the food out of
the fridge, put it on the grand piano in the
living room, switched off the fridge and
closed the door to the living room, and that
was it till the spring: our own ridiculously
outsized walk-in larder.

That building no longer stands. A little
while ago, I walked past where it used to
be, and to my surprise and momentary
disorientation I found that the whole
block, which had housed some shops,
possibly a bank, certainly a pub, and our
flat as well as several others, was simply
gone. I imagine a new office block,
or mixed residential and commercial
development is going up on the site. This

used to be owned by the Crown Estate, I imagine it still is.

Our landlady though was an American poet who had been living in London for about twenty years by then, who had six grown up children, and who was not only subletting individual rooms to us flat sharers, but also ran the small music rehearsal studios downstairs, called St Alban's Street Studios; and when these were fully booked, musicians would sometimes come up to our flat and use the grand piano in the living room to practise.

I loved living there; it felt in an almost old-fashioned sense 'bohemian,' I was still new to town, and this was a place with an unbeatable location, directly behind Piccadilly Circus, in a tiny street wedged in between Lower Regent Street and Haymarket, used mostly by taxis to change direction in the one way system, or as a shortcut. (But not every London cab driver knew of it, even though it was so central it was undoubtedly part of 'The Knowledge.' On one occasion, I had one who was so surprised that there was a street in the West End he'd never heard of that he switched off the meter and let me guide him to my doorstep, just to find out...)

The terms of the lease on the flat stipulated that our landlady was not actually allowed to sublet any part of it, but was meant to use it solely for herself and her family. It can't have been long after this, my final audio diary entry, that we were told she was going to lose the flat, unless she could convince a judge that we were not really renting our rooms from her, but living there on a friendly basis, in a quasi artistic arrangement. This was utter nonsense, of course, even though two of our flatmates had, at times, been staffing the reception of the studios downstairs, for one pound an hour...

No wonder, therefore, our feeble attempts at making our tenancies sound like anything other than what they were, without perjuring ourselves in court, got absolutely nowhere, and soon the decision was made for me: I had to move out, as the Crown Estate took back the property. (Ironically, a full quarter century later, the same landlady got into trouble again with her neighbours, over the flat where she had actually been living all this time. Also over subletting rooms, now on *AirBnB*. Again there was a court case. Again she lost...)

On The Tape, apart from sensing a move come on, I also "feel I have to change jobs just for the sake of diversity"—by which I probably mean variety—"and getting to

know something new," by which I probably
mean learning it.

I record, and relate, that there's "no hurry
about that, although first initiatives
will start now towards the end of the
year." Other than that, I now have "lots
to do regarding Edinburgh next year,"
and apparently I had been doing some
workshops on Tuesdays prior to the trip,
because I now tell myself that these are
starting up again. Perhaps I'll even "enrol
for the City Lit course."

The City Lit course was a then well
known—almost in a small way legendary—
part time acting course; legendary not
so much perhaps for the content or
the teaching (though it was led by two
inspiring and much loved Canadians), but
for the fact that admission was granted on
a purely first come, first served basis, rather

than through auditions, which meant that people quite literally queued up overnight to get in. I obviously followed through on this, because I certainly did queue up all through the night, two years running, and I met in that queue people I'm still friends with today, one of whom built from scratch first the Southwark Playhouse and then Arcola Theatre, two respected London Off West End theatres today, at both of which I've had plays of mine staged.

The final note of this holiday, I hear myself say, "is summarised perhaps in the word 'fantastic,'" by which I mean not so much that it had been exciting—although it had—but that I had met really good people, among them many friends of friends; that I had been able to stay with people all the way through except in Edinburgh and Paris; and that I had loved being with people I knew and knew really well.

I end The Tape by telling my future self that I had just been on a walk through St James's Park, after coffee at the ICA, and that it now feels "a bit like decision time." It's a time of looking back and of looking forward, and if this was a break in-between, then the part that starts now is going to be a busy one: "I feel quite determined to finish my studies; I feel determined to do Edinburgh next year. I won't apply for drama school, I'd rather finish the evening studies first."

This is a degree I was taking, at what was then known as the Polytechnic of Central London and has since been renamed University of Westminster. In Social Sciences. I've always held this to be the most useless degree imaginable, but it was a valuable time all in its own right, and it turned out to be far from useless, but for reasons I could not really have foreseen.

Clearly, though, it was simply an extension of my general education, rather than in any way a vocation, since my heart was then already firmly on theatre, whence it has rarely ever really strayed. But the earliest possible moment therefore for me to go to a full time drama school would be "next year," while in the meantime "I'll try to do a City Lit course;" and everything else, I declare, is up for grabs.

It was, I say in the most languid voice that I've ever heard anyone, including myself, say anything, and that now brings one more smile at myself of back then to my lips, "a totally invigorating and satisfying experience. I feel very grateful for having been able to do this, and for having been received with such hospitality and friendship."

Finally, I reckon that there's "a lot of travelling to do" (which I do, over time), and "a lot of living in different places," too, naming Paris and Italy as likely contenders, which is something I haven't done: after St Alban's Street I crashed with friends in Hackney for a short while, then I lived near Marble Arch for a few years, then in Ashley Gardens near Victoria in precisely the flat that our former landlady has since also lost (though that block is unlikely to be torn down any time soon, as it is a gorgeous residential two-tone brick building, in keeping entirely with the Westminster Cathedral, which stands directly next to it, and probably listed).

After that I moved into The Anthony in Earl's Court, where I've been living ever since. Always London: maybe the first and certainly the longest love of my life...

Printed in January 2023
by Rotomail Italia S.p.A., Vignate (MI) - Italy